THIS JOURNAL BELONGS TO:

MOM

DAUGHTER

Name:

Name:

....

....

We start this yourney with:

This journal is a shared journey for mother and daughter. It's more than just a place for questions and answers - it's a space for strengthening your bond, sharing dreams, and discovering each other!

How does it work?

Find time for each other - Choose a moment when you can sit down together and have a relaxed conversation. It could be once a week or whenever you feel like it.

Ask each other questions - Each page contains questions for both mom and daughter. Answer honestly, write, draw - enjoy the process!

Open up for dialogue - Every answer leads to a conversation, bringing you closer together. It's a time to connect, understand, and support one another.

Do this together:

Plan fun activities - Use the space in the journal to write down things you'd love to do together. Whether it's a movie night, a walk, or a weekend trip!

Get creative - Draw, add photos, stickers - make each page unique and special, just like your relationship!

This is your journal, your story. Enjoy every moment together!

OUR BUCKET LIST

Let's make a list of 10 things we want to do together before we graduate from middle school

Mom's Top 10

1.

2.

3.

4.

5.

6.

7.

8.

9.

10.

My Top 10

1.

2.

3.

4.

5.

6.

7.

8.

9.

10.

Circle the ones you like best on the other person's list. Choose which ones you can implement this year and develop a plan to implement them:

THINGS I LOVE

5 things mom loves about me

1.

2.

3.

4.

5.

5 things I love about my mom

1.

2.

3.

4.

5.

MY FAVORITE THINGS

Here are some of our favorite things...

	MOM	ME
Favorite TV show		
Favorite friend's		
Favorite color		
Favorite teacher		
Favorite thing in my room		
Favorite game to play out		
Favorite game to play ins		
Favorite song		
Favorite meal		
Favorite vacation		
Favorite sleeping position		
Favorite thing to do when I need "alone" time		

IF I COULD GO ANYWHERE IN THE WORLD....

MOM

I would go here:

I'd be with:

I would do these things there::

ME

I would go here:

I'd be with:

I would do these things there::

TEN QUICK QUESTIONS

	MOM	ME
Last thing I ate:		
I will never, ever, ever eat:		
I cannot live without my:		
I cannot live without my:		
Best day of the week:		
When I amsad, this makes me feel better:		
Last person who made me laugh:		
Best time of the day:		
Song that is Stuck in my head:		
The outfit that is currently on repeat:		
My favorite subject at school s/was:		

WOULD YOU RATHER...

	MOM	ME
Be really strong or really fast?		
It be Halloween or Easter?		
Eat ice creamor cake?		
Be too hot or be too cold?		
Be an eagle or a cheetah?		
Be able to fly or be invisible?		
Ride a bike or ride a camel?		
Swimin the ocean or in a pool?		
Only be able to whisper or to yell?		
Be able to breathe underwater or read people's minds?		
Build a snowman or a sandcastle?		
Live in a big city or a small town?		
Spend the night camping or in a hotel?		

THREE WISHES

If I had three wishes, I would wish for these things

MOM'S WISHES FOR ME:

FOR MY FAMILY:

FOR THE WORLD:

MY WISHES FOR MYSELF:

FOR MY FAMILY:

FOR THE WORLD:

IF I HAD A DAY OFF AND COULD DO WHAT I WANTED,

MOM

I WOULD...

ME

IF I COULD BEINVISIBLE, I WOULD,

MOM

I WOULD...

ME

WHAT DO YOU DO DURING A TYPICAL DAY WHEN I'M AT SCHOOL?,

MOM

I WOULD...

ME

IF WE SWITCHED ROLES FORA DAY,
I'D BE MOST EXCITED TO DO THIS:

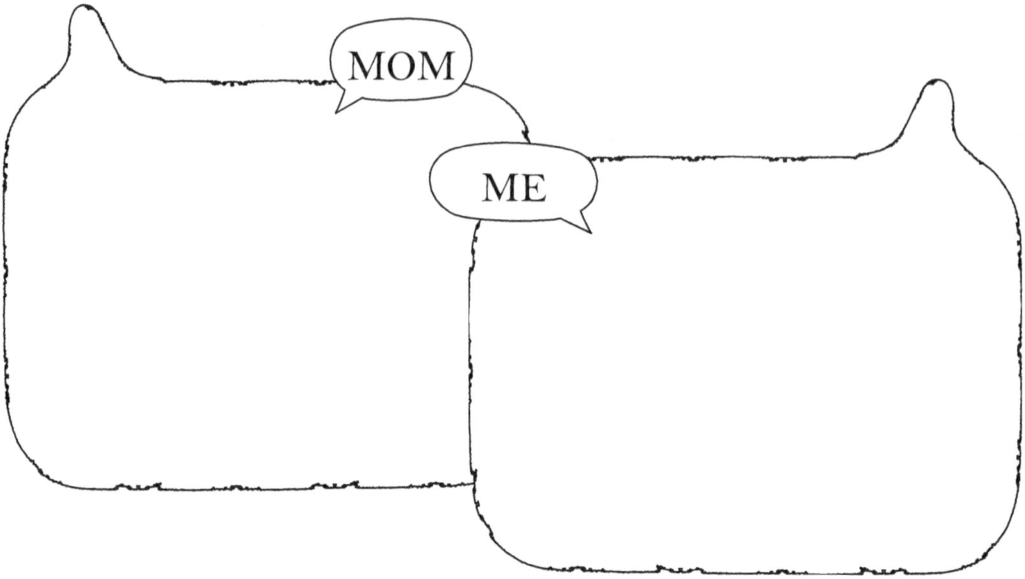

And least excited about:

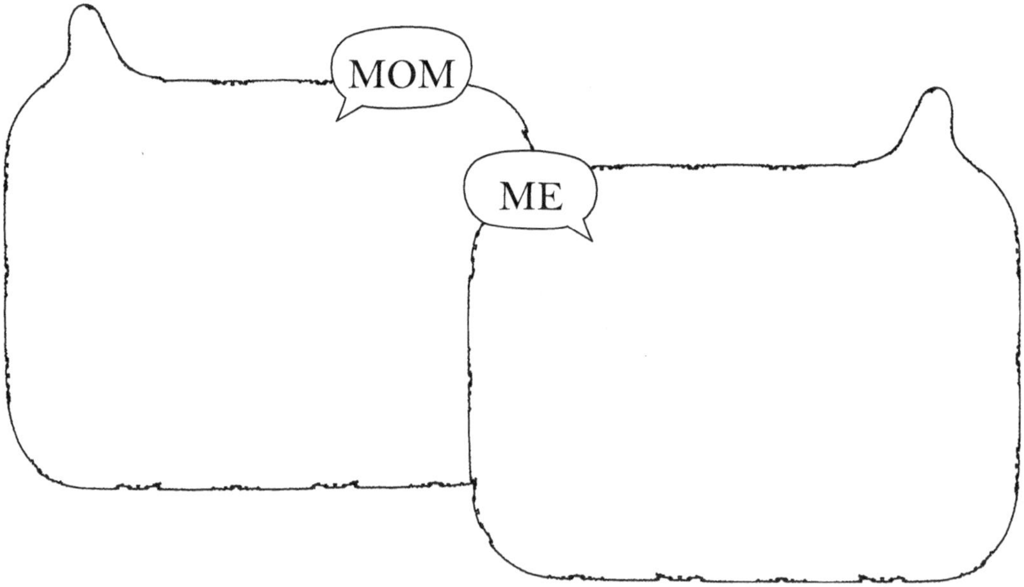

I THINK WE'RE REALLY SIMILAR BECAUSE…

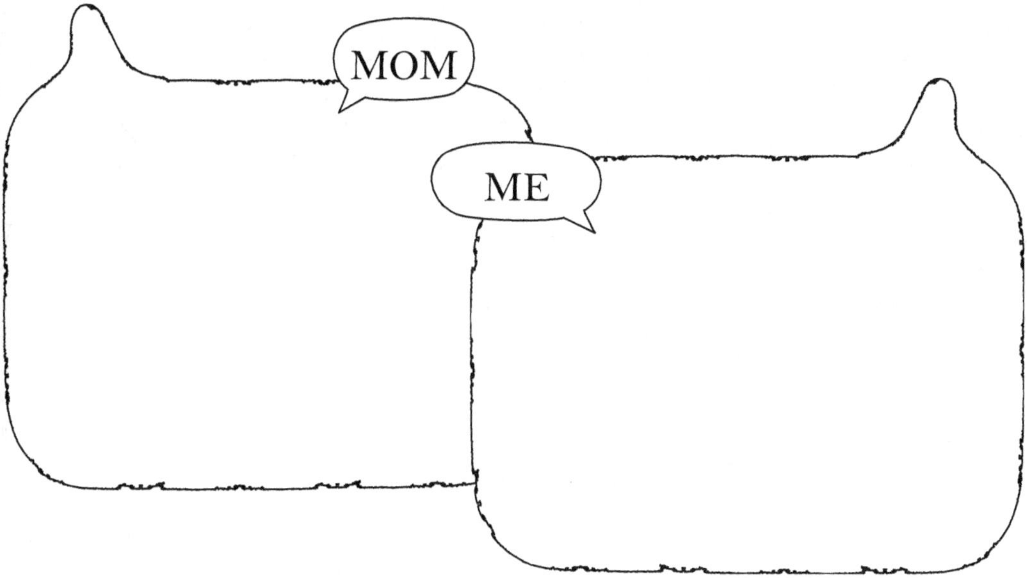

I think we're different because…

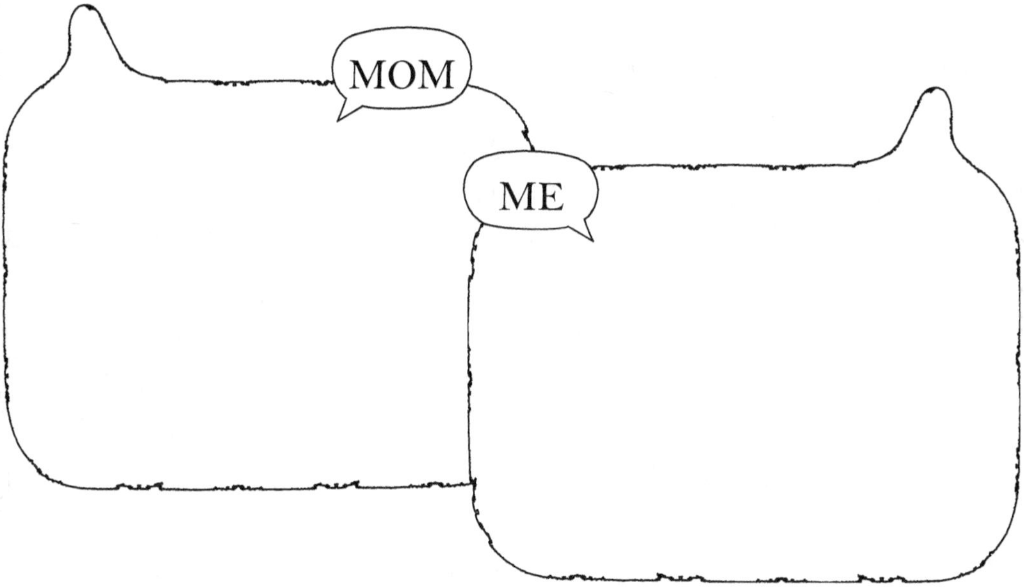

MY FAVORITE THINGS TO TALK TO YOU ABOUT ARE:

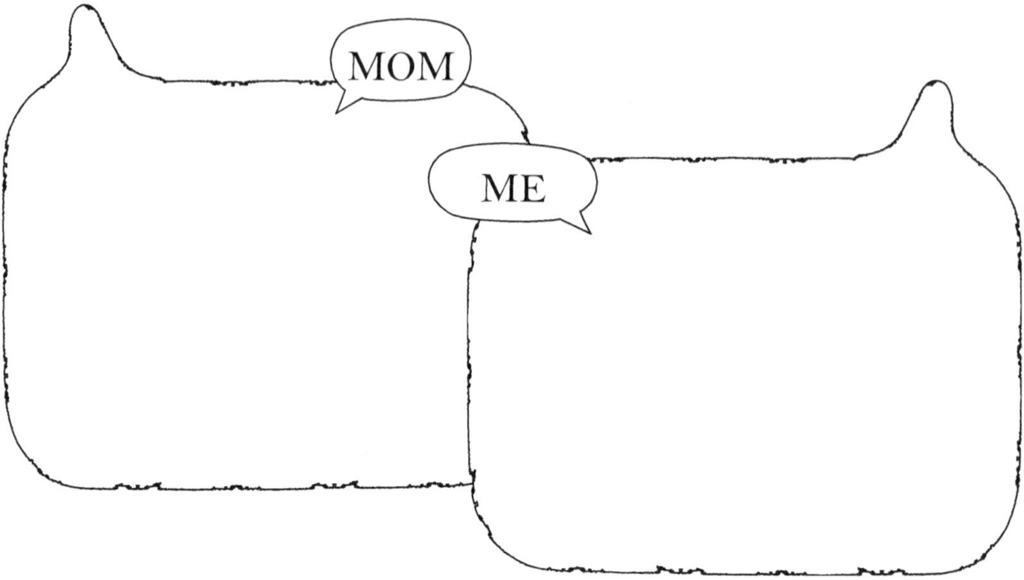

I find it really hard to talk to you about:

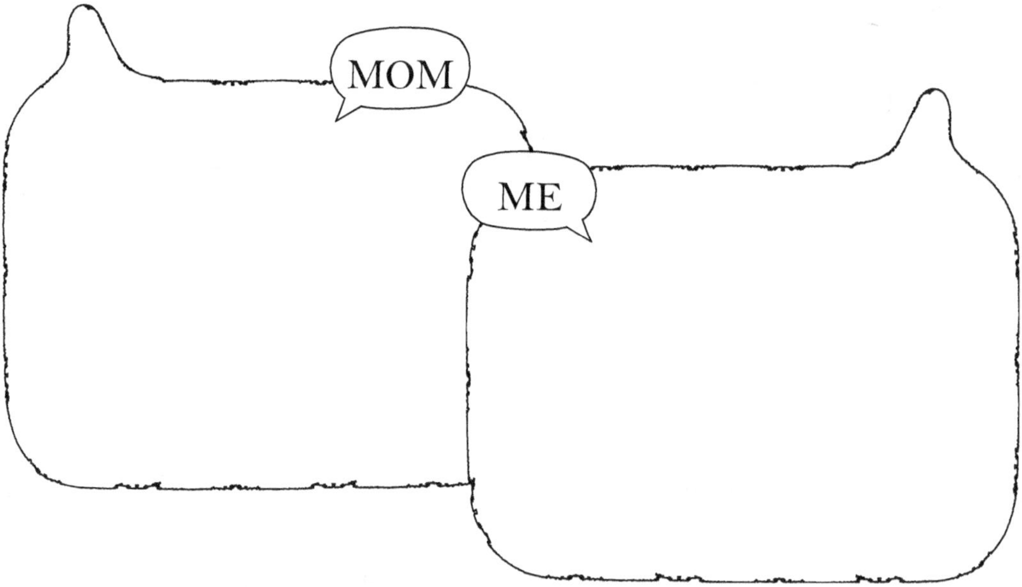

YOU MAKE ME FEEL SPECIAL WHEN…

MOM

ME

WHEN YOU WERE MY AGE, WHAT DID YOU LIKE TO DO?

MOM

ME

If I were agrown-up I'd do these things differently:

SOME THINGS THAT WORRY ME ARE…

MOM

Answer Here:

ME

Thoughts/questions on the answer above:

SOME THINGS THAT WORRY ME ARE…

ME

Answer Here:

MOM

Thoughts/questions on the answer above:

SOMETIMES I CAN'T SLEEP BECAUSE I'M THINKING ABOUT…

MOM

Answer Here:

ME

Thoughts/questions on the answer above:

SOMETIMES I CAN'T SLEEP BECAUSE I'M THINKING ABOUT…

ME

Answer Here:

MOM

Thoughts/questions on the answer above:

I WISH I COULD DO THIS WITH YOU MORE…

ME

Answer Here:

MOM

Thoughts/questions on the answer above:

I WISH I COULD DO THIS WITH YOU MORE…

MOM

Answer Here:

ME

Thoughts/questions on the answer above:

I WISH YOU'D HELP ME MORE WITH...

ME

Answer Here:

MOM

Thoughts/questions on the answer above:

I WISH YOU'D HELP ME MORE WITH…

MOM

Answer Here:

ME

Thoughts/questions on the answer above:

I FEEL THE MOST LOVED WHEN…

ME

Answer Here:

MOM

Thoughts/questions on the answer above:

I FEEL THE MOST LOVED WHEN…

MOM

Answer Here:

ME

Thoughts/questions on the answer above:

I WISH KNEW HOW TO…

ME

Answer Here:

MOM

Thoughts/questions on the answer above:

I WISH KNEW HOW TO…

MOM

Answer Here:

ME

Thoughts/questions on the answer above:

I WISH PEOPLE KNEW THESE THINGS ABOUT ME:

ME

Answer Here:

MOM

Thoughts/questions on the answer above:

I WISH PEOPLE KNEW THESE THINGS ABOUT ME:

MOM

Answer Here:

ME

Thoughts/questions on the answer above:

SOMEONE WAS MEAN TO ME BECAUSE THEY DID/ SAID THIS:

ME

Answer Here:

My reaction was:

It made me feel:

MOM

Thoughts/questions on the answer above:

SOMEONE WAS MEAN TO ME BECAUSE THEY DID/ SAID THIS:

MOM

Answer Here:

My reaction was:

It made me feel:

ME

Thoughts/questions on the answer above:

I FELT SO PROUD OF MYSELF WHEN…

ME

Answer Here:

MOM

Thoughts/questions on the answer above:

I FELT SO PROUD OF MYSELF WHEN…

MOM

Answer Here:

ME

Thoughts/questions on the answer above:

I GET NERVOUS WHEN…

ME

Answer Here:

MOM

Thoughts/questions on the answer above:

I GET NERVOUS WHEN…

MOM

Answer Here:

ME

Thoughts/questions on the answer above:

TODAY I WANT TO COMPLAIN ABOUT…

ME

Answer Here:

MOM

Thoughts/questions on the answer above:

TODAY I WANT TO COMPLAIN ABOUT…

MOM

Answer Here:

ME

Thoughts/questions on the answer above:

THE WORST THING HAPPENED AT SCHOOL/WORK/HOME TODAY…

ME

Answer Here:

MOM

Thoughts/questions on the answer above:

THE WORST THING HAPPENED AT SCHOOL/WORK/HOME TODAY…

MOM

Answer Here:

ME

Thoughts/questions on the answer above:

I JUST HAVE TO GET THIS OFF MY CHEST…

ME

Answer Here:

MOM

Thoughts/questions on the answer above:

I JUST HAVE TO GET THIS OFF MY CHEST…

MOM

Answer Here:

ME

Thoughts/questions on the answer above:

TODAY I WANT TO TELL YOU SOMETHING THAT'S BEEN ON MY MIND…

ME

Answer Here:

MOM

Thoughts/questions on the answer above:

TODAY I WANT TO TELL YOU SOMETHING THAT'S BEEN ON MY MIND…

MOM

Answer Here:

ME

Thoughts/questions on the answer above:

THE MOST EMBARRASSING THING THAT'S EVER HAPPENED TO ME IS...

ME

Answer Here:

MOM

Thoughts/questions on the answer above:

THE MOST EMBARRASSING THING THAT'S EVER HAPPENED TO ME IS…

MOM

Answer Here:

ME

Thoughts/questions on the answer above:

WHEN I GROW UP, I WANT TO BE…

ME

Answer Here:

MOM

Thoughts/questions on the answer above:

WHEN I WAS LITTLE, I WANTED TO BE...

MOM

Answer Here:

ME

Thoughts/questions on the answer above:

MOM, I HAVE A QUESTION FOR YOU:

(write your question below)

RESPOND HERE

MOM

______________ ,I HAVE A QUESTION FOR YOU:

Child's Name

(write your question below)

RESPOND HERE

ME

DRAWING PAGES

Draw a picture of your mom – make sure to include lots of details and labels!

Draw a picture of your child – make sure to include lots of details and labels!

MOM

DRAWING PAGES

Start drawing a picture, but don't finish!
Pass it on and have the other person complete it.

DRAWING PAGES

Draw a picture of your dream vacation

MOM

ME

DRAWING PAGES

Draw how you feel today.

DRAWING PAGES

Draw a picture of how you would give your room a make-over. Include lots of details and labels!

MOM'S ROOM

MY ROOM

DRAWING PAGES

Draw a picture of yourself as a superhero.
What's your superpower?

MOM

ME

DRAWING PAGES

Draw yourself in your most favorite place in your house.

MOM

ME

DRAWING PAGES

Think about your upcoming birthday. Draw a picture and write about what you want to do on your birthday or for your birthday party. Who's there? What does your cake look like? Where would you go?

MOM

ME

DRAWING PAGES

What would your "best day ever" look like? Draw a picture and explain.

MOM

Where would you go? Who would you be with?

ME

DRAWING PAGES
Draw what it feels like to be:

ME

HAPPY

SAD

ANGRY

SCARED

DRAWING PAGES
Draw what it feels like to be:

HAPPY

MOM

SAD

ANGRY

SCARED

Use these additional pages if you need more space for your answer.

Use these additional pages if you need more space for your answer.

Use these additional pages if you need more space for your answer.

Use these additional pages if you need more space for your answer.

Use these additional pages if you need more space for your answer.

Use these additional pages if you need more space for your answer.

Use these additional pages if you need more space for your answer.

Use these additional pages if you need more space for your answer.

Use these additional pages if you need more space for your answer.

Use these additional pages if you need more space for your answer.

www.ingramcontent.com/pod-product-compliance
Lightning Source LLC
LaVergne TN
LVHW020120090726
842905LV00041B/1110
* 9 7 8 8 3 6 8 2 9 4 0 6 4 *